Max's Christmas

Max's Christmas
ROSEMARY WELLS

A Puffin Pied Piper

For Beezoo Wells

PUFFIN PIED PIPER BOOKS
Published by the Penguin Group
Penguin Books USA Inc., 375 Hudson Street, New York, New York 10014, U.S.A.
Penguin Books Ltd, 27 Wrights Lane, London W8 5TZ, England
Penguin Books Australia Ltd, Ringwood, Victoria, Australia
Penguin Books Canada Ltd, 10 Alcorn Avenue, Toronto, Ontario, Canada M4V 3B2
Penguin Books (N.Z.) Ltd, 182-190 Wairau Road, Auckland 10, New Zealand
Penguin Books Ltd, Registered Offices: Harmondsworth, Middlesex, England

Originally published in hardcover by
Dial Books for Young Readers
A Division of Penguin Books USA Inc.

Library of Congress Catalog Card Number: 85-27547
Printed in Hong Kong by South China Printing Company (1988) Limited
First Pied Piper Printing 1994
ISBN 0-14-054563-8

A Pied Piper Book is a registered trademark of
Dial Books for Young Readers, A Division of Penguin Books USA Inc.,
® TM 1,163,686 and ® TM 1,054,312.
3 5 7 9 10 8 6 4 2

MAX'S CHRISTMAS
is also available in hardcover from
Dial Books for Young Readers.

Guess what, Max!
said Max's sister Ruby.
What? said Max.

It's Christmas Eve, Max, said Ruby,
and you know who's coming!
Who? said Max.

Santa Claus is coming,
that's who, said Ruby.
When? said Max.

Tonight, Max, he's coming tonight!
said Ruby.
Where? said Max.
Spit, Max, said Ruby.

Santa Claus is coming right down
our chimney into our living room,
said Ruby.
How? said Max.

That's enough questions, Max.

You have to go to sleep fast,
before Santa Claus comes, said Ruby.

But Max wanted to stay up
to see Santa Claus.
No, Max, said Ruby.

Nobody ever sees Santa Claus.
Why? said Max.
BECAUSE! said Ruby.

But Max didn't believe a word
Ruby said.

So he sneaked downstairs...

and waited for Santa Claus.

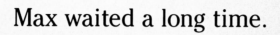

Max waited a long time.

Suddenly, ZOOM! Santa
jumped down the chimney
into the living room.

Don't look, Max! said Santa Claus.
Why? said Max.
Because, said Santa Claus,
nobody is supposed to see me!

Why? said Max.
Because everyone is supposed to be asleep in bed, said Santa Claus.

But Max peeked at Santa anyway.
Guess what, Max! said Santa Claus.
What? said Max.

It's time for me to go away
and you to go to sleep,
said Santa Claus.
Why? said Max.

BECAUSE! said Santa Claus.

Ruby came downstairs.
What happened, Max? asked Ruby.
Who were you talking to?
Where did you get that hat?

Max! Why is your blanket
so humpy and bulgy?

BECAUSE! said Max.